PURR-FECT PETE

SAMANTHA HAY

Illustrated by
CHRIS INNS

For Alice and Archie S.H.
For Fiona, a spectacular act C.I.

KINGFISHER

First published 2008 by Kingfisher
an imprint of Macmillan Children's Books
a division of Macmillan Publishers Limited
20 New Wharf Road, London N1 9RR
Basingstoke and Oxford
www.panmacmillan.com

Associated companies throughout the world

ISBN 978-0-7534-1647-1

Text copyright © Samantha Hay 2008
Illustrations copyright © Chris Inns 2008

The right of Samantha Hay to be identified as the
author of this work has been asserted by her in accordance
with the Copyright, Designs and Patents Act 1988.

1 3 5 7 9 8 6 4 2
1TR/1207/WKT/SC(SC)/IISMA/C

A CIP catalogue record for this book is available from the British Library.

Printed in China

Contents

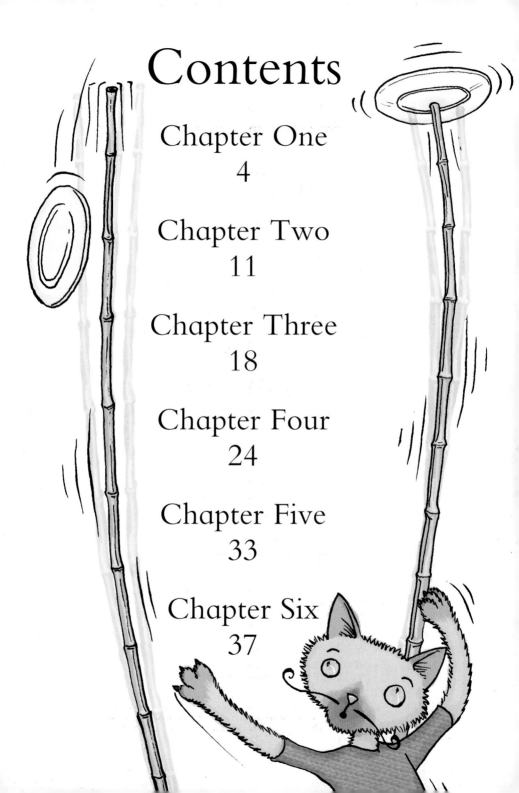

Chapter One

When High-Wire Wilma fell and
broke her tail, everyone said the Flying
Fur Balls were finished!

The Flying Fur Balls
were the best
acro-cats
in the world.
And Wilma
was the star
of their show.

She was as brave
as a lion.

She was as light
as a kitten.

She could leap and twirl.
Tumble and whirl.

6

Back flip . . .

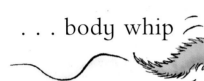

. . . body whip

. . . and balance on
absolutely anything.

But one night it all went wrong.

Wilma had a wobble.

She was walking

the wire, when she

tripped and

fumbled.

Then tumbled . . .

. . . and crashed to

the ground.

Wilma quit!

"It's no good," she told the rest of the
Flying Fur Balls. "I've used up eight
of my nine lives, it's time to hang up
my leotard!"

The Flying Fur Balls were aghast!
"But what about us?" they cried.
"We can't do acro-catics with just
four of us!"

Wilma shrugged.
"You'll need to look for a new member!"

Chapter Two

So they did.

The Flying Fur Balls

held an audition.

And every acro-cat

in the land went along.

"The cat we choose will need to be tough!" growled Gloria, the strongest of the Fur Balls.

Gloria had the strength of ten cats and was always at the bottom of acro-cat towers, which was just as well, because Gloria liked to scoff salami sandwiches, and had the most awful bad breath.

"The cat we choose will need to be small and springy," said Chin and Chen, who were terrific tumblers.

"And brave as a lion!" said Brenda, who was a super stilt-walker.

But the trouble was they couldn't find any cat who measured up. "We might as well pack up and go home!" sighed Brenda as the last would-be Fur Ball was sent away with his tail between his legs. Then suddenly there was a pattering of tiny feet and the smell of stinky cheese . . .

14

The door crashed open and there stood
a very small kitten.

Brenda put on her glasses. "I don't
think you're old enough to audition."

The tiny cat didn't
answer. Instead he
did a handstand.

"Not bad," said
Chin and Chen.
"But have you got a spring in your step?"

The tiny cat leapt
in the air and
somersaulted
twice before
landing.

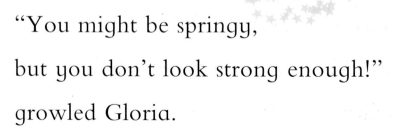

"You might be springy,
but you don't look strong enough!"
growled Gloria.

The tiny cat cart-wheeled over, scooped Gloria up, and twirled her above his head. Then he back flipped onto the wall bars, scrambled to the top, and dangled Gloria down by her tail. "You're hired!" they all shouted together.

Chapter Three

The tiny cat was called Pete.

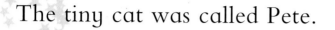

He was as brave as
a lion, and as light
as a kitten.

He could leap
and twirl.

Tumble and whirl.

Back flip . . .

. . . body whip

. . . and balance on
absolutely anything.

He fitted in
pu**rr**-fectly!

When Brenda did her amazing stilt-walking, plate-spinning spectacular, Pete stood on her shoulders spinning cups of cream.

When Chin and Chen did their world-famous super-sonic tornado tumbles Pete joined in too, cart-wheeling wildly until the audience felt dizzy watching him.

And when Gloria whizzed round the ring on her motorbike, driving it with her toes, Pete stood on her head and juggled milk bottles!

The Flying Fur Balls were a sell out.

And everyone agreed Pete was

pu**rr**-fect!

Well . . . apart from some rather

peculiar habits.

He never
ate fish.

He hated

cream.

And he liked to snack on stinky cheese.

And strangely, he didn't know any

good mouse jokes.

But the Flying Fur Balls didn't mind . . .

until one terrible night.

Chapter Four

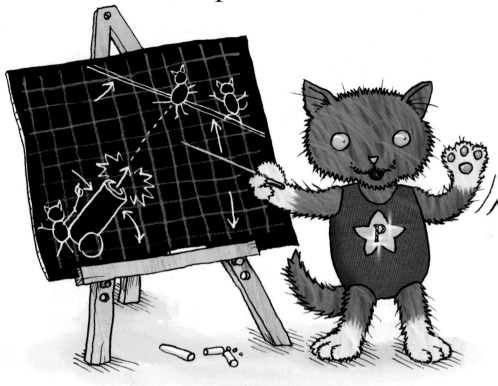

It had been Pete's idea.

"I know," he'd suddenly squeaked, during rehearsals. "Why don't we try something really spectacular. Why not fire me out of a cannon, right up on to the high wire – without a safety net!"

Brenda's
eyes popped.

Chin and
Chen gulped.

Gloria gasped.
It was the most
daring idea ever.

And they all agreed to try it out

that night . . .

The big top was full. Hundreds of

cats were packed in like sardines

to see the show.

"Ladies and

gentlemen!"

boomed Brenda,

standing on top

of the cannon.

"Tonight – Fur Ball Pete will attempt the bravest feat . . ."

Pete took a bow.

"He'll cannonball on to the high wire without a safety net!"

The audience gasped as Pete climbed into the cannon.

Brenda lit the fuse.

There was an almighty bang . . .

a flash of orange . . .

and Pete shot out of the cannon, like a

giant cork bursting out of a bottle.

Amazingly, he landed

right on target,

in the middle of the high wire.

The audience went berserk. Meowing

and yowling and tossing their boxes of

tuna fish popcorn into the air

with delight.

Fur Balls!

Pete, now balancing on the high wire,

beamed and waved, and didn't wobble

even slightly.

But then Chin sniffed.

"What's that burning smell?"

Chen looked at Pete and gasped,

"He's on fire!"

Pete certainly was.

His fur had started to smoulder when

he'd been shot out of the cannon.

Now it was covered in flames!

It looked like the end for Pete . . .

But it wasn't.

He suddenly did a very peculiar thing.

He grabbed at his fur, zipped open

his tummy, then took all his

skin off!

"Frozen fish bones!" gasped Gloria.

"Pete's a mouse!"

Chapter Five

Pete was

indeed a mouse.

A chunky grey mouse,

with long whiskers and a pink tail.

He tossed the burning cat costume

away and stood shivering on the

high wire.

Everyone was shocked and stunned.
Then suddenly a yowl from the
audience went up:
"EAT HIM!"

Pete peered down at the
angry cats helplessly.
Then something whizzed
past his ears.
It was a box of tuna
fish popcorn.
The audience had
started throwing their
show snacks at him!
Another box narrowly
missed him . . .

And then . . .

Thwack!

One bashed him square

on the head, and Pete

wobbled . . . and fumbled . . .

and tumbled.

"Ahhhhh!" he squeaked, as he

crashed down towards the ground.

He covered his eyes and waited for

the splat. But it never came.

Just as he was about
to hit the ground, a
giant pair of paws
reached up and
caught him.
Pete gasped.
It was Gloria.
"P-p-p-p-please
don't eat me,"
he squeaked, smelling
her hot salami breath.

Chapter Six

But Gloria didn't eat him. Instead, she
turned to the yowling audience and let
out a loud growl.

"Listen you lot! This mouse is the best acro-cat I've ever worked with,"
"He may not actually be a cat," she added, "but I think Pete is purr-fect!"
The audience started spitting and hissing.

Gloria glowered at them, "And if any of you want to eat Pete – you'll have to eat me first!"

The hissing and spitting stopped.

"And us too," yowled Chin and Chen.

Brenda sighed. "And me too,

I suppose," she said.

The audience shuffled uncomfortably.

"Right then," Gloria said, "let's get on
with the show."
And amazingly, the Flying Fur Balls
and Pete carried on with their
performance.

Much later, when the show was over and the Fur Balls were back in their dressing room, Pete apologized.

"I didn't mean to trick you," he squeaked. "But I've always wanted to be a Flying Fur Ball!"

Gloria shrugged. "But now everyone knows you're a mouse, you'll have to leave. You don't want to end up being someone's show snack!"

Pete nodded sadly.

But Brenda smiled, "Not so fast.
I have a plan."

The very next day the Flying Fur Balls
announced Pete's retirement.

Then they secretly took him off to a
fancy dress shop and bought him a
new cat costume.

And a few days later, the Fur Balls announced the arrival of a new member of their troop: a kitten called Pedro.

Pedro looked remarkably like Pete. He was the same size and shape. He didn't like fish or cream and he didn't know any good mouse jokes. And he was always snacking on stinky cheese.

But unlike Pete, he never,
NOT EVER, not for all the stinky
cheese in the world, suggested that he
should climb into a cannon, and be
fired on to the high wire!

About the Author and Illustrator

Samantha Hay worked in television for ten years before leaving to start a family and write children's books. Sam lives in Scotland and is the author of *Creepy*  *Customers* and *Hocus Pocus Hound*, also in the *I Am Reading* series. "Even if I could find a cat costume big enough, I don't think I'd be brave enough to follow Pete onto the high wire. I'd be much happier being Gloria – standing at the bottom of the Fur Ball towers."

 **Chris Inns** is an exciting author and illustrator of novelty and picture books. Chris lives in Sevenoaks, Kent with his wife and two young children. "My cat Lizzie is far too lazy to be one of the Flying Fur Balls," says Chris, "but I know she would like to be in the audience eating tuna fish popcorn!"

Tips for Beginner Readers

1. Think about the cover and the title of the book. What do you think it will be about? While you are reading, think about what might happen next and why.

2. As you read, ask yourself if what you're reading makes sense. If it doesn't, try rereading or look at the pictures for clues.

3. If there is a word that you do not know, look carefully at the letters, sounds and word parts that you do know. Blend the sounds to read the word. Is this a word you know? Does it make sense in the sentence?

4. Think about the characters, where the story takes place, and the problems the characters in the story faced. What are the important ideas in the beginning, middle and end of the story?

5. Ask yourself questions like:
    Did you like the story?
    Why or why not?
    How did the author make it fun to read?
    How well did you understand it?

Maybe you can understand the story better if you read it again!